Bunny Trouble

ANIMAL ARK

Bunny Trouble

Lucy Daniels

With special thanks to Janet Bingham

For Thomas

ORCHARD BOOKS

First published in Great Britain in 2018 by The Watts Publishing Group

1 3 5 7 9 10 8 6 4 2

A CIP catalogue record for this book
is available from the British Library.

ISBN 978 1 40835 416 2

Printed and bound in Great Britain by CPI Group (UK) Ltd, Croydon, CR0 4YY
The paper and board used in this book are made from wood from responsible sources.

Orchard Books
An imprint of
Hachette Children's Group
Part of The Watts Publishing Group Limited
Carmelite House
50 Victoria Embankment
London EC4Y 0DZ

An Hachette UK Company
www.hachette.co.uk
www.hachettechildrens.co.uk

CONTENTS

CHAPTER ONE

Amelia Haywood leaned into the car and gave her dad a hug.

"Be good for Mum and Gran," said Dad. "And if you can't be good …"

"… be careful!" Amelia finished, and Dad chuckled. Amelia was still getting used to not living with Dad any more.

After the divorce, he had stayed in their old house in York, while Amelia and Mum had moved in with Gran in the countryside. He always said the same thing when he said goodbye to her.

Dad ruffled Amelia's long, blonde hair. "See you Saturday after next," he said. "Good luck at school. You'll be fine."

Amelia's stomach squirmed. Her first day at her new school was tomorrow.

After Dad had driven away, Amelia turned towards the red front door of her new home. There was a hawthorn tree by the porch, with a blackbird pecking at the feeder that hung there. Bees were crawling hungrily over a clump of lavender. After a weekend in York, with its crowded city streets and bustling shops, it felt strange to be back in the countryside and among all the animals again.

Amelia opened and shut the front door quietly, so she wouldn't disturb the blackbird, and went back into the kitchen. Gran was clearing away the

tea things and Mum was sitting at the
table, chopping vegetables for dinner.
They smiled as Amelia walked in, and
she grinned back. Gran and Mum
looked so alike. Gran's hair was short
and neat, while Mum's was long
like Amelia's, but they had the same
laughing blue eyes.

Blue eyes like mine, thought Amelia.
Dad always said she looked like Mum.

"Tell us more about your weekend,"
Mum said. "It sounds like you and Dad
had a great time."

"It was really cool," Amelia said. "The
best bit was going to the cinema. I missed
Welford, though – and the kittens!"

She and her new friend Sam had
found the newborn kittens in Sam's
garage, without their mother. But they
had managed to find her and reunite
the little family, just in time to save the
tiny kittens. The cat family were now
staying at Animal Ark, where the vets
were looking after them until the kittens
were old enough to leave their mother.

"Can I go and visit them?" asked
Amelia. "I'll go to Sam's on the way
and see if he wants to come too."

Gran glanced out of the window. "You
won't have to do that. Here's Sam now!"

Amelia grinned. Through the window,
she saw her friend and Mac, his Westie

puppy, coming up the garden path.
She rushed to open the door.

Mac scrabbled at her knees, yapping
happily and wagging his stubby tail.
"Hi, Sam!" said Amelia. "Hello, Mac!"
She knelt to stroke Mac's thick white
coat and rub his pointed ears.

Sam's dark brown eyes were shining with excitement. "Hey, Amelia!" he said. "I think Mac missed you. Do you want to come and see the kittens with us?"

Amelia laughed. "Definitely! Come on – I can't wait to go to Animal Ark again!"

CHAPTER TWO

Outside Animal Ark, Mr Hope the vet was saying goodbye to a woman with an excitable cockapoo. The cute little dog had a plastic cone around its neck.

"Buster will need to wear it until his stitches have healed," Mr Hope was saying. When he noticed Amelia, Sam and Mac, he waved. "Hello! You must have come to see the cat family. Come on in!"

They followed Mr Hope into the surgery reception area. Amelia glanced round, thinking how strange it looked on a Sunday, with all the empty chairs and nobody sitting at the reception desk. Magazines were piled neatly on a side table, and the walls were covered in posters with information for pet owners. The one nearest the door showed two black and white rabbits. It said, "WANTED: new home for two adorable rabbit sisters!" Amelia smiled. The rabbits looked very cute.

"You can leave Mac in here," said Mr
Hope, "while we're in the hotel."

"Stay, Mac," said Sam, looping the
dog's lead over one of the hooks on the
wall. Mac flopped down, his wagging
tail thumping the floor. Sam patted his
head. "Good boy!"

Mr Hope led them through to the
"hotel", the cosy back room where
poorly animals were kept if they
needed to stay overnight. There were
large, comfortable pens at floor level
and smaller ones on top. In one of the
bottom ones, an old, grey-muzzled dog
with a bandaged leg opened one eye
and closed it again.

Mrs Hope, the other vet at the surgery, was leaning over one of the pens. Her kind face lit up when she saw Amelia and Sam. "Come and look," she said.

Amelia felt excitement bubble up inside her as they peeped into the pen. Caramel, the mother cat, was lying on her side on a padded, heated cushion. She purred happily as she looked up at Amelia and Sam. Her four kittens were lying beside her, drinking her milk. Three of them were tortoiseshell, like their mother, and the fourth was ginger. Their tiny paws kneaded her soft tummy, and every now and then one gave a soft, contented squeak.

"They've grown so much since we found them," said Sam.

Amelia nodded. "Even the little ginger one." She shivered, remembering how the ginger kitten had almost died when they first found them.

"Caramel is looking after them very well," said Mrs Hope.

"How long do the kittens have to stay with her?" Sam asked.

"Until they're at least eight weeks old," Mrs Hope replied. "So about another six weeks."

Amelia and Sam shared a glance. Amelia knew he was thinking the same thing as her: *Six weeks to find all the kittens homes.* They had rescued Caramel from Mr Stevens's farm, and he had agreed to adopt her and one of the tortoiseshell kittens, who he'd named Snowdrop because of the white tip on her tail. But the other three kittens still needed owners, and Amelia was determined to find them.

And then, she thought dreamily, *maybe Mr and Mrs Hope will let me help out at Animal Ark all the time.* The two vets had told her she wasn't old enough yet, but Amelia could think of nothing she wanted more in the whole world.

"But there's lots to do before the kittens leave Caramel," Mr Hope went on. "We need to start handling them, and playing with them every day. They have to learn to be comfortable around people while they're tiny. Then they'll become good pets."

Amelia's heart leapt. This was another chance to prove themselves! "We can play with them, can't we, Sam?" she said.

Sam nodded hard. "Definitely! We'll come every day after school."

"Wonderful!" Mrs Hope said. "With your help these kittens will grow up into perfect pets."

One of the tortoiseshell kittens stopped feeding. She rolled away from Caramel and pushed herself up on her wobbly legs. "Oh!" said Amelia. "Her eyes have opened now! They're so blue!"

"Kittens' eyes open about a week after they're born," said Mr Hope. "They'll change colour too before long. In fact, young kittens change every day! This little lot are just starting to try to walk, but they'll be running around soon.

Perhaps now is a good time to start handling them." He opened the mesh front of the pen and stroked Caramel's head. Then he picked up a tortoiseshell kitten and gave her to Amelia.

Amelia felt a burst of joy. She could feel the kitten's firm little body underneath the soft fur, and the cushiony pads of her tiny feet. The kitten bumped her head against Amelia's thumb and snuffled the palm of her hand. Amelia stroked her tiny ears. They weren't pointed yet like Caramel's, but folded over. She put a finger against the kitten's mouth and was rewarded with a lick of the little rough tongue.

Sam was cradling the other tortoiseshell kitten. "Holding them is like magic," he whispered. Amelia nodded in agreement.

Mrs Hope cuddled the ginger kitten, and Mr Hope picked up Snowdrop. Caramel watched, blinking her eyes with contentment.

After a little while, they gently put
the four kittens on a soft mat on the
floor. With shaky steps, the tiny things
wobbled towards each other. Mrs Hope
found a piece of string, and waggled
it between them. The kittens swiped at
it with their tiny paws, but they soon
flopped down, yawning.

"Time to go back to Mum," said
Mrs Hope.

Amelia helped scoop up the kittens
and carefully put them back in the pen.
Caramel began washing them, purring
loudly in time with the strokes of her
tongue. The kittens curled up around
her and went to sleep. Amelia hugged

herself with happiness.

"They'll be ready to play again tomorrow," Mrs Hope said.

Amelia laughed. "We'll be here!"

They went back to the reception area. "I hope Mac's been good," Sam said. But as he swung open the door, he let out a gasp. Mac was nowhere to be seen!

"Mac!" Sam called. "Where are you?"

They looked under all of the chairs, and at last found Mac lying under the reception desk, behind the bin. He was chewing something black and shiny. Amelia reached under and grabbed him around his soft tummy, hauling him out, and Sam wrestled the thing from

between Mac's sharp
puppy teeth.
It was a high-
heeled shoe.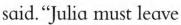

"Oops," Sam
said. "Julia must leave
her work shoes under her desk at the
weekend." He looked closely at the shoe.
"Luckily it's not damaged, just a bit
slobbery!" He rubbed the receptionist's
shoe dry on his hoodie and put it back
under the desk.

"Phew! We found him just in time!"
said Amelia.

Sam nodded. "Let's get him home
before he chews anything else!"

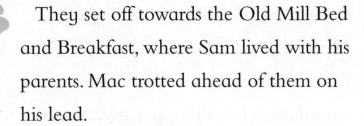

They set off towards the Old Mill Bed and Breakfast, where Sam lived with his parents. Mac trotted ahead of them on his lead.

"How's his toilet training going?" Amelia asked.

"Really well. He hasn't peed indoors all weekend. But instead he's been chewing everything." Sam's face fell. "He's made a hole in the doormat. Mum and Dad are really cross about it."

Amelia felt a knot of worry twist inside her. She knew Sam's parents had told him that if he couldn't train Mac properly, he would have to give the puppy up – they couldn't risk a naughty

puppy driving away the B&B's guests.

Sam's shoulders were slumped.

"Don't worry," Amelia said, trying to sound as cheerful as possible. "We'll train him. He's going to be the best behaved dog in the village."

Sam did his best to smile. "Thanks. So are you looking forward to school tomorrow?"

Amelia sighed. "I don't know … I've been trying not to think about it. What's it like?"

"It's fun – for school, anyway," Sam said. "You'll be in my class, remember?"

Amelia nodded. "I'm glad we're friends already."

"Me too," Sam said. "But don't worry, everyone's really nice."

That's what Dad said, Amelia thought. But worry still fluttered inside her like a flock of birds. *I hope they're both right!*

CHAPTER THREE

The following morning, Amelia stood nervously by the whiteboard at the front of her new classroom. Her teacher, Miss Hafiz, was wearing a pretty lilac headscarf and a smart jacket. She had very kind eyes and a clear, gentle voice. Amelia thought she seemed nice.

"Class," she said, "meet Amelia. She's come to join us. Say hello, everybody."

The entire class stared at Amelia. "Hello," they chorused.

Like her old classroom, there were several tables with pupils sitting around them. At the back of the room was a glass tank with some logs and plants inside. Amelia's stomach fluttered with nerves. But then she spotted Sam's

friendly face, and she felt a little better.

"Welcome, Amelia," Miss Hafiz said. "Why don't you tell us something about yourself?"

Amelia rubbed the back of one leg with the toe of her other shoe. "Um…" She couldn't think of a single thing. Sam caught her eye and gave her an encouraging grin. "Well, I … er … I love animals."

Miss Hafiz said, "In that case, I think you'll get on well with Izzy. Here, take this seat next to her."

Amelia sat where Miss Hafiz had shown her. Izzy glanced at her from under her fringe and then looked away.

"Take out your maths books," Miss Hafiz said. "Amelia, you can share with Izzy for now."

The four other kids at the table began chattering to each other, taking no notice of Amelia. Izzy pushed the book towards Amelia without looking up. *Maybe she's shy*, thought Amelia.

She noticed Izzy's pencil case was decorated with a guinea pig, and there were rabbit stickers on her maths book. "These are cool," Amelia said, pointing at the stickers.

"Thanks," said Izzy, but that was all.

Amelia chewed her lip. *Miss Hafiz is wrong. Izzy doesn't like me at all!*

As she and Izzy started working in
silence, Amelia thought about Chloe,
her best friend at her old school. Chloe
had sent her a message the night
before, with a picture of her and their
other friends, Natalie and Alex, having
a sleepover. They were all grinning
happily at the camera, wearing
matching animal onesies.

Amelia sighed. For a moment, she felt very lonely. *I wish they were here now*, she thought.

The class settled down to work. After maths, they did a spelling game. The morning seemed to go very slowly, and Amelia longed for breaktime.

At last Miss Hafiz said, "Listen, everybody. Your homework for this week is to design your perfect house. What is it made of? What does it look like? Think hard."

Everyone started talking at once. A red-haired boy sitting at Amelia's table said, "I know who lives in their perfect house – Mrs Cranbourne.

It looks like it's haunted!"

The other kids laughed, but Amelia noticed that Izzy wasn't even smiling.

"Who's Mrs Cranbourne?" Amelia asked the red-haired boy.

"You'll know her when you see her," he replied.

The other boy at the table said, "Thomas is right. She's scary!"

One of the girls nodded. "She looks like a witch!" The girl pulled an evil face and cackled.

They must be making this up, Amelia thought, but she couldn't help giggling.

The bell rang for breaktime. Everyone rushed for the door, but Sam pushed his way through the crowd towards Amelia.

"Hey, Amelia!" he said. "It's my turn to feed the geckoes. Do you want to help me?"

Amelia grinned. "Definitely!"

The geckoes were in the glass tank she'd spotted at the back of the class. Above the tank was a sign with information on it. *This tank is called a vivarium,* Amelia read. *Did you know that geckoes have millions of tiny hairs on their feet? These hairs mean they can walk anywhere – even upside down!*

As Sam slid back the tank's lid, she felt the warmth of the heat mat inside. There was a water bowl, plants, a climbing branch and a dark, cave-like nest box, but no geckoes.

He rattled a packet of mealworms, and something moved inside the nest box. Sam dropped a few of the mealworms into the tank, and Amelia was startled to see them wriggle.

"They're alive!" she exclaimed with a shudder. "Yuck!"

"Gross, isn't it?" said Sam. "You'll get used to it, though."

Amelia pulled a face, but made herself watch. "I want to be a vet when I grow up, and I bet Mr and Mrs Hope have to see gross things all the time."

A moment later, a little pointed face poked out of the box. It had bright eyes

 and a pale, fluttering throat. The gecko darted forward on splay-toed feet. It snapped up a mealworm and chewed with steady chomps.

"Here comes the other one," Sam whispered, as a second gecko came out of the nest box. Amelia saw its pink tongue flash out as it pounced on a mealworm. The geckoes looked alike. They both had bumpy, sandy skin patterned with dark splodges. "They're called leopard geckoes," Sam said, and Amelia could see why.

"What are their names?" she asked.

"Draco and Lucius. They're almost fully grown."

"They're so cool," Amelia said.

When the geckoes had eaten, Sam closed the vivarium lid carefully, and they went outside for break. The playground backed on to a playing field that seemed to go on for ever. The tarmac was painted with number games, and it was full of laughing, chattering, running kids. Amelia suddenly felt nervous again.

Sam asked, "So, what do you think? Miss Hafiz is nice, isn't she?"

Amelia nodded. "But Izzy doesn't like me. She won't talk to me."

"That's weird," Sam said. "Izzy's usually really friendly." He looked around the playground. "There she is, by the football goal."

Izzy was leaning back, one foot flat against the wall behind her. Her head was down and her hands were shoved in her pockets. No one was with her.

"Is she always on her own?" asked Amelia. She remembered the pang of loneliness she'd felt earlier, when she'd thought about her old friends' sleepover.

Sam shook his head.

"Maybe something's wrong," said Amelia. "I wonder what it could be?"

After school, Amelia hurried home to eat her dinner with Mum and Gran, then went over to the B&B to see Sam.

"Are you all right, Amelia?" asked Sam. They were standing in the hall, Sam clipping on Mac's lead. "You seem a bit quiet."

Amelia sighed. "Today's been sort of weird," she said. "Going to school made me think about my old friends. I really miss them, and they're having loads of fun without me."

"We'll have fun too," said Sam.

"I know," Amelia said with a smile. Mac barked and licked her hand.

"Mac says he's your friend," Sam said.

"Thanks, Mac," said Amelia, laughing. She kneeled down to pat Mac's fluffy head. "You're a lovely friend," she told the puppy.

"Izzy was just in a bad mood," said Sam. "Why don't we ask her to come with us to see the kittens? If there is something wrong, stroking them might cheer her up."

"Good idea," said Amelia.

Sam held a rubber bone in front of Mac's nose. "Hey, Mac, look what Dad bought you. You can chew it on the way. Better than shoes, right?"

The puppy looked up at Sam and gave a questioning yip.

Amelia laughed. "I don't think he understands!"

Sam sighed. "He only wants to chew things he shouldn't!"

They had to go by the duck pond to get to Izzy's house. They were walking past it when they saw an elderly woman in a purple jacket riding a

bicycle, its basket filled with shopping. Her long scarf had come loose, and was trailing out behind her. As she rode past them along the path, Mac suddenly pounced at the scarf, snapping at it with his jaws.

"Get off, you silly dog!" shrieked the woman.

Sam shouted, "Mac, no! Don't try to chew that!" and made a lunge for the puppy.

The woman reached to yank back her scarf, and the bike swerved on the muddy pavement. Mac let go of the scarf and Sam scooped him up. The bike hit the kerb and its back wheel flew up.

"Aaahhhh!" With a yell, the woman lurched over the handlebars.

Amelia felt like she was watching a slow-motion video. She could see what was going to happen, but she couldn't do anything to stop it …

The woman's scarf fluttered as she toppled straight into the pond.

SPLASH! She landed on her bottom, waist-deep in slimy green pond-water.

SPLASH! Her shopping bag landed beside her. A startled duck quacked and flapped away.

"Oh no!" Amelia cried. She and Sam ran to the edge of the pond.

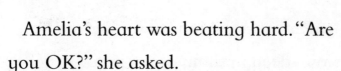

Amelia's heart was beating hard. "Are you OK?" she asked.

Sam held out his hand. "Can we help you?"

The woman struggled awkwardly to her feet. She ignored Sam's hand and almost fell over again as she sploshed up the bank, water dripping off her and leaving a puddle on the path. "That … that … that dog is a MENACE!" she fumed.

Sam took a step back. "I'm sorry …" he began.

But the woman was still shouting. "That naughty dog has RUINED my shopping!"

50

Sam hugged Mac
close. The puppy's
ears drooped, and
Amelia thought
they both looked
as if they wanted to
run away.

"We're really sorry," Amelia said.
"Mac didn't mean it. I'll get your stuff."

She kicked off her trainers and
socks and waded into the cold water.
Pondweed gathered round her legs, and
her toes squelched in the mud. *Urgh!*
She grabbed the canvas bag and hauled
it back on to land, then held it out to
the woman.

"Sorry it got wet," said Amelia.

The woman gave a snort. She wrestled her bike upright, snatched the dripping bag from Amelia, put it back in the basket and started pushing her bike down the road.

"That," whispered Sam, "is Mrs Cranbourne."

Amelia blinked in shock. "Whoa!" she murmured. "So she really is scary!"

Mrs Cranbourne looked back at them over her shoulder. "That puppy had better stay away from me," she called. "Or else!"

CHAPTER FOUR

Izzy's house was in the middle of a row of terraced houses. Amelia knocked on the door while Sam pulled Mac away from a pot of geraniums he was trying to eat.

The door opened. Izzy stood there, frowning at them.

Maybe this wasn't a good idea after all,
Amelia thought.

"Er, hi, Izzy," she said. "We were just
wondering if—"

To her surprise, Izzy's face crumpled
and she burst into tears. Amelia glanced
at Sam, whose eyebrows were raised
in confusion.

"What's wrong, Izzy?" Amelia asked.

"It's Tulip!" sobbed Izzy.

"Who's Tulip?"

Izzy gulped. "My rabbit. I've been
really worried about her. And now …"
She gave another sob. "She's gone
missing!"

So that's what was wrong, Amelia

thought, suddenly realising why Izzy had been unfriendly.

Amelia put an arm around Izzy. "We'll help you find Tulip, won't we, Sam? When did you last see her?"

Izzy wiped her eyes. "She was in her hutch when I came home from school."

"So she can't have gone far," Sam said. "Where's her hutch?"

Izzy led them through the house. The back garden was mostly taken up by a large shed and a little patch of lawn. A rabbit hutch in the corner was attached to a short chicken-wire run on the grass.

"What does Tulip look like?" Amelia asked Izzy.

"She's black and white. She's really pretty, with black patches on her eyes and ears, and a white flash down her nose to her chin." Izzy sniffed as she opened the doors to show them the empty hutch. Mac whined and rubbed against Izzy's legs, as if he was trying to comfort her. Izzy crouched down and hugged him close.

Amelia and Sam studied the hutch.
It had big doors at the front, and a
small sliding door at the side, which led
directly into the run.

"I left this one open," said Izzy,
pointing to the sliding door, "so Tulip
could go on the grass."

"So she must have escaped from her
run," Amelia said. She kneeled down,
studying the chicken wire. There was

a small hole in the ground beneath it.
"Look! It's a tunnel!"

"So Tulip dug her way out!" Sam said.
"We need to find more clues." He picked
up Mac and held him towards the hutch.
"Mac, this is Tulip's hutch. Take a big
sniff!" He turned to Izzy and Amelia.
"If he gets her scent, he might sniff out
where she went. Look! He's off!"

Mac squirmed out of
Sam's arms and dashed
across the garden.
Amelia felt a burst of
hope as they watched the
excited puppy.

Mac skidded to a stop – at the neatly coiled hosepipe. Then he started chewing the end.

Sam groaned and pulled him away. "No, Mac!"

Amelia gave a sigh of disappointment. She looked around the small garden. There was a pair of plastic chairs, a stone bird bath – and a pile of freshly dug earth beside the wooden fence …

"Hey," she said. "Another tunnel! Tulip must have dug her way out of the garden!"

They hurried back out through the house. "I'm not supposed to go out without telling Mum," said Izzy, "but she's

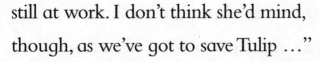

still at work. I don't think she'd mind, though, as we've got to save Tulip …"

She led Amelia and Sam along the terraced street and on to a path that ran behind the row of gardens. They found the back of Izzy's fence with the other end of Tulip's tunnel beneath it.

"So where did Tulip go next?" Amelia wondered out loud.

The path was bare earth, stamped down by passing feet, with clumps of green leaves here and there. The garden fences were on one side, and a hedge ran along the other. One lonely apple tree grew beside it. Amelia looked around its trunk. *Nothing!*

Izzy was running up and down frantically. "She isn't here!" she cried. "What if we can't find her? She'll be so frightened!"

Amelia tried to comfort her. "We haven't looked everywhere yet—"

"Look," Sam interrupted. "These leaves have been nibbled."

Amelia looked more closely at the clumps of weeds by the fence. They had nodding yellow flowers and round seed-heads. "Dandelions!" she said. "Rabbits like them, don't they, Izzy? Do you think Tulip could have eaten these?"

Izzy nodded, her face a little more hopeful. Quickly, they searched through

the dandelions, looking for the rabbit.

"There are more eaten ones here,"
shouted Sam.

"And here," said Amelia. "We're
following Tulip's trail!"

Suddenly Izzy pointed to a cluster of
shiny brown balls beside the hedge on
the other side of the path. "Fresh rabbit
droppings! They could be Tulip's!"

"We must be close," said Amelia.
"Keep looking!"

They searched the path. They found
more droppings, and then a patch of
earth with claw-marks. It looked as if
something small had scratched its way
under the hedge into the next garden.

Amelia grinned. "Tulip must have hopped under here! All we have to do is ask the owner if we can look for her."

But to her surprise, Izzy's eyes went wide in alarm. Sam held up his hands and shook his head. "No way!" he said.

Amelia frowned. "Why not?"

"Because it's Mrs Cranbourne's house!"

Amelia groaned. Standing on tiptoes, she peered over the hedge. There was a mass of weeds and brambles. The top half of a sprawling house loomed at the far end of the garden.

Curtains were drawn across the upper windows, and the walls were smothered by ivy. Near the chimney pots, a weather vane creaked in the gentle breeze. Amelia swallowed. *Thomas was right*, she thought. *It does look like a haunted house …*

"What if Mrs Cranbourne finds Tulip?" said Izzy, her voice trembling.

"We'll just have to find her first, won't

we?" Amelia fought down her nerves and poked around in the hedge, pulling apart two branches to make a small gap.

"Come on, we can squeeze through!"

Sam frowned. "I don't know …"

"We don't have a choice," Amelia said. "It'll be dark soon, and Tulip won't be able to find her way home."

Izzy swallowed and looked worried. "What if a fox gets her?"

"I don't think Mrs Cranbourne will let us go into her garden," said Amelia, "so we'll have to sneak in. We won't touch anything of hers – she'll never know we were here."

"I guess, if Tulip's in danger …" said Izzy.

"Exactly," said Amelia. "I bet it's what Mr and Mrs Hope would do." In fact, she was sure of it. The Hopes would do anything to help an animal – and so would she!

"All right," said Sam at last. He tied Mac's lead to the tree and crawled through the gap in the hedge. Izzy followed, and Amelia went last, shuddering a little as twigs caught her clothes and tangled in her hair. Sharp thorns scratched her skin. A moment later she stood with the others in Mrs Cranbourne's garden.

They crept through it. Straggling nettles swayed over their heads, and brambles caught at their ankles. Amelia pulled her clothes free, wincing as the thorns dug into her fingers, then stepped past a holly tree. Izzy and Sam followed.

She stopped in surprise. This part of the garden wasn't overgrown at all. It was planted with rows of fruit and vegetables.

"Tulip would absolutely love this!" whispered Izzy.

Amelia nodded. "Maybe we'll find her in here!"

They began to search. Amelia edged down rows of tomato plants covered in small, yellow, star-shaped flowers. She reached a patch of rhubarb, and lifted each of the big, fan-shaped leaves. Then she crouched down to search among the

strawberry plants – and gasped.

There was a soft, quivering nose.

Amelia parted the leaves carefully. A small black and white rabbit was sitting nibbling a ripe strawberry.

Tulip!

Amelia leaned in very slowly, being careful not to scare her. Gently she put her hands under the rabbit's chest and bottom and lifted her up. Tulip let the strawberry drop from her mouth. Her black ears swivelled. There was red strawberry juice on her white chin and her soft fur tickled Amelia's nose. Tulip planted her white-socked feet on Amelia's chest. They felt very strong.

"Izzy!" Amelia called, as
loudly as she dared.

Izzy turned and gave a yelp
of delight. Amelia handed her
Tulip, and Izzy buried her
face in the rabbit's fur.
"Oh, Tulip! Don't ever
run away again!"

Sam was grinning.
"Now we just need to sneak back out!"

"WOOF!"

They all spun towards the sound.
The hedge rattled. The nettles quaked.
And Mac burst out of the grass, his lead
trailing behind him.

"Mac, no!" cried Sam.

But instead of running to Sam, the puppy headed straight for the house. Amelia's stomach flipped over. Mrs Cranbourne would see them!

They gave chase. Brambles snagged their clothes, but they didn't stop until they'd caught up with Mac. He'd reached the back of the house. There was a cat flap in the door, and to Amelia's horror, the puppy rammed his nose against it. Mac bounced back on to the doormat with a howl of surprise. He lay there shaking his head. Amelia almost laughed.

Then the door flew open. Mrs Cranbourne stood in the doorway, hands on hips. Her face was red with fury.

"What are you doing in my garden?"
she shouted. She stared at Amelia and
Sam, and then she turned to Izzy.
Her eyes dropped to Tulip, with her
juice-stained fur, and she drew in a
sharp breath.

"So that's who's been eating my
strawberries!" Mrs Cranbourne shouted.

Amelia opened her mouth to explain, but Mrs Cranbourne took a threatening step towards Izzy and Tulip. "THIEF!"

Amelia knew they had to escape. "Run!" she cried.

CHAPTER FIVE

They dashed back towards the hedge.
At first Amelia couldn't see the hole
they'd scrambled through. She felt a
shiver of panic.

But Sam shouted, "This way!" and
Amelia saw him vanish into the hedge,
pulling Mac's lead behind him. Izzy

went next, clutching Tulip. Shaking with relief, Amelia dived into the hedge and scrambled through.

Sam and Izzy were already racing down the path. Amelia dashed after them, past the back of Izzy's house and round the corner. They finally stopped at the main road.

Amelia clutched her side. "Whoa," she panted, half laughing now that it was all over. "That was close!"

But Izzy gave a cry of dismay. "Oh! What's happening to Tulip?"

Amelia and Sam gathered round her. Tulip was lying limp, panting fast, with her eyes half closed.

Sam gasped. "She seems really ill!"

"Let's get her to Animal Ark," said Amelia. "Hurry!"

"Hmm," said Mrs Hope, carefully feeling Tulip's tummy with her gloved hands. Amelia, Sam and Izzy were gathered around the table in the consultation room at Animal Ark, watching anxiously. "I can see Tulip's feeling poorly," the vet said. "Can you tell me what she's been up to?"

Together, they explained what had happened. "Then we found her in, um, a strawberry patch," finished Amelia.

"It sounds like Tulip's had quite an adventure," said Mrs Hope. "It's the strawberries that are making her ill."

"Are strawberries bad for rabbits?" Izzy asked.

"Sadly, yes," said Mrs Hope. "Rabbits

love strawberries, but they upset their tummies. They should eat mainly hay." She stroked Tulip's ears. "Don't worry, Izzy, she's just got a tummy ache – it'll get better by itself. Just make sure she has lots of fresh water in her hutch. How is she otherwise?"

"Well …" Izzy touched Tulip's back paw, where there was a bald spot. "She chews her paw a lot. I don't know why."

Mrs Hope studied Tulip's paw. "How big is her run?" she asked, rubbing cream into the patch of bare skin.

"About this long," said Izzy, holding her arms wide. "My mum made it specially. She's a carpenter."

Mrs Hope put Tulip back in her carry basket. The little rabbit crouched down, her eyes closed.

"What's really wrong with Tulip is that she's bored," Mrs Hope said. "If you can make her home more interesting, she won't chew her paw – and she won't escape in search of excitement, either. Do you think you can manage that?"

Izzy nodded. "I would do anything for Tulip!"

"And we'll help you!" said Amelia. "Won't we, Sam?"

"Course we will," said Sam.

"Well, good luck!" said Mrs Hope, giving Izzy a prescription for more paw

cream. "I'm sure you can do it."

As they went through to visit the kittens, Amelia felt a swell of pride. This was another chance to help an animal – and to show the Hopes just how useful she could be at Animal Ark.

After school the next day, Amelia and Sam went to see the kittens, then joined Izzy in the shed in her garden. Mac sat at their feet.

The shed walls were hung with saws, screwdrivers and chisels. There were shelves, too, full of boxes overflowing with nuts and bolts. In the middle of the

shed was a workbench, and the floor
was stacked with wooden planks and
poles, and rolls of chicken-wire. They'd
told Izzy's mum about Tulip, and she'd
suggested they make her a new house.
Izzy was really excited. She'd been
so nice at school that Amelia hadn't
thought as much about Chloe and her
other old friends.

"Tulip's much better now," said Izzy.

"That's great!" said Amelia. "I can't
wait to get started on her new home."
She shared a secret grin with Sam. Last
night they had come up with a special
surprise for Izzy, and Amelia couldn't
wait to see her reaction. Mac gave

an excited yelp and tried to close his
mouth around a wooden block.

"No, Mac," Sam said sternly. "You
mustn't chew anything in here!"

"Hi, kids." Izzy's mum came inside.
She was wearing overalls and her
hair was pulled up into a messy bun.
"Now listen to me." She looked very
serious. "Before we get started, Mrs
Cranbourne came round earlier. She
was complaining about you three, and
a certain puppy and rabbit, being in
her garden yesterday. So, tell me – what
have you been up to?"

They all looked at each other guiltily.
Amelia took a deep breath. "We know

we shouldn't have, but Tulip got into her garden, and we had to rescue her."

"Mrs Cranbourne's so scary," added Izzy, "we didn't think she'd let us get her back."

Izzy's mum frowned. "Did you try asking her first?"

They shook their heads.

"Well, maybe you should have," said Izzy's mum. "She might be nicer than you think."

Amelia caught Sam's eye, and guessed he was thinking the same thing as her. *Izzy's mum doesn't realise how mean Mrs Cranbourne is!*

Izzy's mum put a tin of pencils and some paper on the workbench. "Let's get on with making Tulip's new run. Let me know when your design's ready!"

She went back into the house, and they each grabbed a pencil. "There isn't enough space to make the hutch wider, but we can make it taller," said Amelia.

"Ooh!" said Izzy. "Like a double-decker!"

They all began drawing and chipping in ideas. Before long, they'd designed a brand new home for Tulip.

"She's going to love this!" said Izzy. "What an amazing surprise for her!"

As they took their drawing inside, Sam whispered excitedly to Amelia, "And it's nearly time for Izzy's surprise!"

In the kitchen, Izzy's mum studied the drawing carefully. "Great work, everyone! I'll get on with building it. Meanwhile …" She reached for a carrier bag on the worktop. Mac looked at it hopefully, but Sam grabbed his collar. Izzy's mum took the bag outside and emptied the bag on to the grass. It was full of empty cereal packets and toilet-roll tubes. "Why don't you see if you can make some rabbit toys from this lot?"

They set to work, following an online video that showed them how to make toys by stuffing straw into the toilet rolls. From the shed came the sound of sawing and hammering. Mac sniffed around them, then started chewing on a cereal box.

"Uh-oh," said Sam, pulling it out of the puppy's mouth. "Here, Mac, chew this instead."

Sam pulled the rubber bone out of his pocket and threw it. But Mac took no notice at all. Sam groaned.

"Don't give up," Amelia told him. "We'll get him to stop chewing the wrong things eventually."

"I hope so," muttered Sam. "I can't bear to think of giving him up."

"Me neither," said Amelia. "We'll find a way to stop him, I promise."

An hour later, after a pizza break, Izzy's mum called them over. "What do you think?" she asked.

The new hutch stood before them. It
had two storeys, a fun tunnel winding
around the outside, and ramps for Tulip
to get between the levels. There was a
cosy, closed-off place for her to sleep,
and lots of nooks for hiding snacks for
her to find.

Sam and Amelia high-fived, and Izzy
clapped her hands. "It's perfect!" Izzy
cried. She took Tulip out of her old
hutch. "Come on, Tulip," she said. "Try
out your new home!"

She placed Tulip on the top level. Tulip
sniffed around – then sat down.

"Oh," said Izzy, her face falling.
Amelia felt a pang of disappointment.

"Maybe she just needs to get used to it," said Izzy's mum.

The doorbell sounded from inside the house.

"Who can that be?" said Izzy's mum. She winked at Amelia and Sam.

Amelia's stomach fluttered. *It's the surprise!* She and Sam both jumped up.

Izzy looked puzzled as she followed
them through the house.

Standing on the doorstep was a short
man holding a wicker basket. Two fluffy
black and white noses were poking
through the holes in it. "Hello," said the
man. "I'm Mr Jameson. I'm sorry I'm a
bit late!"

Izzy's mum smiled.
"You're not late at
all. Please come in.
Amelia, why don't
you tell Izzy why Mr
Jameson is here?"

Amelia could hardly
speak for grinning.

"Izzy – meet Tulip's new friends."

Izzy looked very confused. "What do you mean?"

"Surprise!" cried Amelia. "After we went to Animal Ark, I did some research on rabbits. I found out they're much happier if they live with friends."

"And these two rabbits need a new home," said Mr Jameson. He stroked the long ears poking out of the basket. Izzy began to smile.

"Amelia and Sam persuaded me they should come and live here," Izzy's mum said. "What do you think, Izzy?"

Izzy nodded, speechless. She gave her mum a big hug, and then hugged

Amelia and Sam. Mr
Jameson gave her
the basket and said
goodbye, and they all
went into the back
garden.

Izzy opened the
basket. Everyone
gasped at the sight of the two adorable
little rabbits inside. At first they leaped
back nervously, but then the rabbits let
Izzy and Amelia pick them up. They felt
as soft and cuddly as Tulip.

"What do you think you'll call them?"
her mum asked.

Izzy stroked the rabbits thoughtfully.

"Poppy and Rose, to go with Tulip. Poppy's the one with the black splodge on her nose."

Gently, they put the rabbits into Tulip's new hutch. Tulip's ears swivelled up. She turned to stare at Poppy and Rose, her whiskers quivering as she sniffed them.

"Do you think Tulip will like them?" Izzy whispered.

Everyone held their breath, waiting to see what the three rabbits would do ...

CHAPTER SIX

They all watched anxiously as the three
bunnies looked at each other. Tulip's ears
twitched. Her nose snuffled. She took a
small step, then another. Then she darted
forward, hopped up to the new rabbits
and sniffed them. They skipped round
each other and snuffled each other's fur.

Relief flooded through Amelia.

"I think Tulip likes them!" Izzy said, her eyes shining.

"And they like her too," said Izzy's mum. "I think they're all going to be very happy together!"

Sam put some of the toys they'd made into the hutch too. Tulip nudged a toilet roll with her nose, and her ears pricked up when it rolled across the hutch. The toy nudged Poppy's paws, and rolled back to Tulip.

"It's like they're playing football!" laughed Amelia.

They all started when the doorbell rang once more. "Is it Mr Jameson again?" wondered Izzy. "Maybe he's forgotten something …" But when they filed through the house and opened the door, it was Mrs Cranbourne.

She glowered at them. "That rabbit," she said, "has been in my garden again.

This time it's eaten ALL my summer raspberries! Every last one! GONE!" She took a breath. "I just wish Mr Whiskers was around. He'd have chased that rabbit away. If I ever see it in my garden again I'll be making rabbit pie for dinner …"

"Mrs Cranbourne," said Izzy's mum, "please let them explain …"

But Mrs Cranbourne spun on her heel and stomped off down the path.

Izzy's mum closed the door. "She does seem upset," she said.

"But it can't have been Tulip," Izzy pointed out. "She's been here with us the whole time." She gave a worried frown. "Do you think she'd really hurt Tulip?"

Amelia and Sam exchanged worried glances.

Izzy's mum shook her head quickly. "Of course not! Why don't you three go and give the rabbits their food and water? I've got some emails to send."

Amelia, Sam and Izzy talked things over while they fed the rabbits. "Do you think Mum's right?" asked Izzy. "Would Mrs Cranbourne hurt Tulip if she found her in her garden again?"

"Even Mrs Cranbourne wouldn't be that horrible," said Amelia. "I think she's just really angry."

Sam looked thoughtful. "She's blaming Tulip for everything."

"Yes," said Amelia. "The only way to stop her from blaming Tulip …"

"… is to find the real thief!" finished Sam. "But how?"

The following day, Izzy had gym class, but Amelia and Sam were on the case! They were sitting in the apple tree beside Mrs Cranbourne's hedge. From up in its branches, they could see Mrs Cranbourne's door beyond the overgrown weeds, and her neat fruit and vegetable patch.

"Now all we have to do is wait for the thief to appear," said Amelia.

Sam nodded. He was holding his mum's phone, which they'd borrowed so they could take photos of what they saw.

They sat quietly in the tree, waiting. Then Sam glanced at Amelia, his face anxious. "Do you still miss your old friends?" he asked.

Amelia thought for a minute, but when she imagined Chloe and the others having a

sleepover, it didn't feel as bad. After all, she was having lots of fun too! "A bit," she told Sam, "but not as much as I did before. Not now I've got Izzy and you and Mac."

Sam grinned. "Well, Mac is pretty great," he said with a laugh.

"It's so nice hanging out with a pet," Amelia said. "Didn't Mrs Cranbourne say she had a cat?"

"Mr Whiskers," remembered Sam.

"That's right. I wonder what he's like."

"Well, if he's anything like Mrs Cranbourne, I bet he scratches and hisses all the time."

Amelia giggled. "Maybe he'll come

out of the cat flap and we'll find out."

They watched for a while, but there
was no sign of a cat.

"You know," said Sam, after a while,
"Mac couldn't get through the cat flap,
could he? It didn't open at all. It must
be locked."

"That's true." Amelia was confused.
"But why would anyone lock a
cat flap?"

They stared at each other, both
realising at the same time.

"Because there isn't a cat living there
any more," said Sam. "Mrs Cranbourne
said she wished Mr Whiskers was
still around."

"He must have died." Amelia felt terribly sad. "Poor Mrs Cranbourne must really miss him."

"Perhaps that's why she's so grumpy," Sam said.

Amelia nodded. They sat in silence. Amelia thought about everything that had happened to Mrs Cranbourne – she'd been knocked into a pond, intruders had appeared in her garden, her raspberries had been stolen, and all the while she was missing her cat … She felt a twinge of guilt.

"Sam," she began – but then something swooped down into the vegetable patch. It was a blackbird.

Amelia gasped. "This could be the thief!"

Sam tapped the phone's camera icon. He zoomed in, holding the screen so Amelia could see it too.

It was a glossy black male, with a bright yellow beak and yellow-edged eyes. He was hopping about on the ground. Then the bushes shook, and Amelia saw a brown female flapping her wings among a spindly redcurrant bush. The branches were too thin for her to perch on. She made a grab for a berry, and then fluttered to the ground. A few berries fell with her. She smoothed her ruffled feathers and began to peck at her prize. The male hopped over to feed on the fallen fruit with her. Amelia was so caught up watching them, she almost forgot why they were there.

Sam turned to her with a grin. "Yes! We've caught the thieves!" Then his grin faded. "I guess we should go and tell Mrs Cranbourne now."

They climbed down the tree and walked up Mrs Cranbourne's overgrown front path and rapped the dull brass knocker. After a long pause, Mrs Cranbourne appeared. When she saw who it was, her face began to go red.

"What are you doing here again?" she snapped. "I told you to stay away!"

"Please, Mrs Cranbourne," Amelia said. "We've got something to show you."

Sam swiped to the blackbird photos on the phone, and handed it to Mrs Cranbourne.

"So," she said slowly, her face softening, "it wasn't the rabbit."

"No," said Sam nervously. "You won't do anything bad to Tulip, will you? Now you know it wasn't her?"

Mrs Cranbourne looked shocked. "Do anything … ? Oh dear." She took her glasses off and rubbed them with a tissue. "I shouldn't have mentioned rabbit pie. I'm afraid I was angry. But I'd never hurt anyone's pet. I love animals, you know."

Amelia felt a wave of relief. And Mrs Cranbourne's apology had given her an idea … "I've been thinking about pets, Mrs Cranbourne. And there's someone I think you should meet …"

CHAPTER SEVEN

"Oh my goodness!" cried Mrs Cranbourne when she saw Caramel and her kittens. "How adorable! May I hold one … ?"

They were in the overnight room at Animal Ark, gathered around the cat family's pen. Mrs Hope gave her a tortoiseshell kitten, and Mrs Cranbourne lifted her up. The deep lines on her face seemed to melt away as she looked into the kitten's blue eyes. Mrs Cranbourne clicked her tongue gently, and the kitten batted a soft paw at her nose.

Sam whispered to Amelia, "I can't believe we were scared of her!" Amelia hid a giggle.

Mrs Cranbourne played with each kitten in turn. Amelia watched closely. "They all like you, Mrs Cranbourne. But I think that first one likes you best. She keeps rubbing your hand!"

"I like her too," said Mrs Cranbourne, stroking the kitten's little ears.

"So what do you think?" Amelia asked. "Would you like to adopt her?"

"She'd keep the birds away from your berries!" added Sam.

Mrs Cranbourne stroked the kitten's fluffy back. "Mr Whiskers used to chase the birds away from my garden," she said. "He passed away nearly a year ago. I still miss him badly."

"I'm sorry to hear that," Mrs Hope said gently. "It's very hard to lose a pet. Do you think you might feel ready to have a new cat?"

"Perhaps." Mrs Cranbourne sounded uncertain. "Of course, I'd have to think of a name for her." The kitten was trying to climb up her arm, and Mrs Cranbourne picked her up again and held her to her cheek. The kitten made a chirruping noise, then purred.

Mrs Hope chuckled. "She really does like you!"

Mrs Cranbourne's face broke into a wide smile. "You're certainly fizzing with energy, aren't you, Miss Fizz?"

Amelia grinned. "That's a great name for her!"

"You've got to adopt her!" said Sam.

Mrs Cranbourne hesitated, then started to laugh. "You're right. Just thinking about taking Miss Fizz home makes me feel better. Yes, please. I would like to adopt her!" She tickled the kitten's nose.

She's not horrible after all, thought Amelia. *She's just lonely, like Tulip was in the hutch on her own.*

"Lovely!" Mrs Hope said. "I'll call you in six weeks, when Miss Fizz is old enough to leave her mum. Then you'll be able to collect her."

Mrs Cranbourne said, "I can't wait! Oh – I nearly forgot. I've brought some of Mr Whiskers' old toys for the kittens." She fumbled around in her big handbag and brought out two tinkly plastic balls, a soft toy mouse and a piece of twisted, knotted rope.

"They'll enjoy those," said Mrs Hope. They put the kittens on the examination table and watched them wobble about, trying to pat the toys and each other's tails. Amelia and Sam made sure they didn't get too close to the edge of the table.

"They're very adventurous kittens," said Mrs Cranbourne.

Mrs Hope nodded. "Sam and Amelia are doing a good job of getting them used to being handled."

Amelia felt warm with pleasure. She and Sam grinned at each other. *Maybe the Hopes will let us help out at Animal Ark one day!* she thought. "We'll find homes for the other two kittens too, Mrs Hope," she said. "I promise."

Mrs Hope smiled. "I know you will."

There was a whine and a thump from the other side of the door. Mrs Hope opened it to reveal Mac yanking on his lead, and Julia holding the other end.

"I'm sorry," the receptionist said. "I've been keeping Mac amused, but he wants to know what's going on in here."

Amelia glanced at the toys the kittens were playing with. She picked up the twisted rope toy. "Mrs Cranbourne, would you mind if we gave this one to Mac?"

"Not at all," Mrs Cranbourne replied.

Amelia waved the toy in front of Mac. The puppy jumped up, catching it in his

mouth. He flung himself on the floor, chewing happily, wagging his tail as if he might shake it off.

"He certainly likes that!" laughed Julia.

Sam was beaming. "We've found a toy he likes to chew at last!" He ruffled Mac's fur. "Mum and Dad will be so relieved! Hopefully he'll stop chewing people's shoes now!"

The rest of the week whizzed by. Soon it was Friday night. Amelia was sitting

on the window seat in her room, with
Sam and Izzy perched on the end of
her bed. Her new friends' sleeping bags
were laid out ready for a sleepover,
and Mac was curled up in his basket,
watching them sleepily.

"Tulip is so much happier now," Izzy said. "She hasn't chewed her foot once since Poppy and Rose moved in. And the new hutch is perfect for them all!"

"That's brilliant," said Amelia.

She reached for the lemonade glass on her desk, and her homework caught her eye. With a little shock, she realised that her drawing of her perfect home looked just like where she lived in Welford! There was the same red front door, the sloping roof, the hanging basket filled with pansies and even the hawthorn tree at the front.

Amelia smiled to herself. She still missed her old home and her old friends at times, but right now she felt very happy in her new home.

And the very best thing about living here, Amelia thought to herself, *is having Animal Ark just up the road!*

The End

Turn the page for a sneak peek at
Amelia and Sam's next adventure!

ANIMAL ARK

Fox Cub Danger

Lucy Daniels

"Can we sh-shout for help?" said Sam through chattering teeth.

Amelia tried to calm her racing heart. "If we shout, we'll scare off the animals. We'll have ruined the search."

Sam groaned. "I wish Mac was here."

So do I ... Of course!

"Sam," Amelia gasped. "You know when Mac found the fox droppings?"

"Y-y-yes ... ?"

"He was following a trail. We must have left a trail of our own when we ran through the woods just now." She glanced around their feet. "Come on, look for a place where the undergrowth is squashed down."

They hunted around the clearing, peering through the moon's faint light for trampled ground. Amelia was looking down so carefully that she almost walked right into a large tree that had branches like fingers reaching out to grab her …

"It's this way!" she said in excitement. "I remember this tree!"

Amelia led the way, picking through the bent fronds and branches and the broken twigs underfoot. Suddenly, she spotted something gleaming on the ground. Bending down, she picked up the object, brushing off the dirt. "My cap!" she exclaimed, feeling a rush of relief. "We're going the right way."

"Look over there!" Sam said.

A wavering torch beam illuminated the trees ahead. Amelia fought the urge to break into a run. She'd never been so pleased to see a torch in her life. She hurried through the trees towards it, Sam close behind.

"Thank goodness!" said Josh's mum. "I was about to start calling for you. We thought you'd got lost."

"We did," Amelia confessed, panting a little. "Any sign of the den?"

"Not yet," said Josh, adjusting his camera. "Let's keep looking."

They carried on walking. Soon

they were in a part of the wood that Amelia hadn't seen before. The path was narrower here, with trees that pressed in on both sides. The leaves rustled like hundreds of whispering voices. And up ahead, they heard a strange, screaming cry – something between a cat's mew and a dog's bark.

Sam yelped. Amelia gasped. "What's that?" she asked, her heart racing. She'd never heard anything like it.

But Josh's mum was smiling at them. "That," she whispered, "is a fox!"

Read **Fox Cub Danger** to find out what happens next ...

Animal Advice

Do you love animals as much as Amelia and Sam? Here are some tips on how to look after them from veterinary surgeon Sarah McGurk.

Caring for your pet

1. Animals need clean water at all times.
2. They need to be fed too – ask your vet what kind of food is best, and how much the animal needs.
3. Some animals, such as dogs, need exercise every day.
4. Animals also need lots of love. You should always be very gentle with your pets and be careful not to do anything that might hurt them.

When to go to the vet

Sometimes animals get ill. Like you, they will mostly get better on their own. But if your pet has hurt itself or seems very unwell, then a trip to the vet might be needed. Some pets also need to be vaccinated, to prevent them from getting dangerous diseases. Your vet can tell you what your pet needs.

Helping wildlife

1 Always ask an adult before you go near any animals you don't know.

2 If you find an animal or bird which is injured or can't move, it is best not to touch it.

3 If you are worried, you can phone an animal charity such as the RSPCA (SSPCA in Scotland) for help.